ATT/CN
P

LUCKY BUNNIES

Sky's Surprise

Hop into
every adventure!

LUCKY BUNNIES

Sky's Surprise

by Catherine Coe

Illustrated by Chie Boyd

SCHOLASTIC

Published in the UK by Scholastic, 2022
Euston House, 24 Eversholt Street, London, NW1 1DB
Scholastic Ireland, 89E Lagan Road, Dublin Industrial Estate, Glasnevin, Dublin, D11
HP5F

SCHOLASTIC and associated logos are trademarks and/or registered trademarks
of Scholastic Inc.

First published in the US by Scholastic Inc, 2020

Text © Catherine Coe, 2020
Inside illustrations by Chie Boyd © Scholastic Inc, 2020
Cover illustration © Andrew Farley represented by Meiklejohn, 2022

The right of Catherine Coe, Chie Boyd and Andrew Farley to be identified
as the author and illustrators of this work has been asserted by them under the
Copyright, Designs and Patents Act 1988.

ISBN 978 1407 18864 5

A CIP catalogue record for this book is available from the British Library.

Printed by CPI Group (UK) Ltd, Croydon, CR0 4YY
Paper made from wood grown in sustainable forests and other controlled sources.

1 3 5 7 9 10 8 6 4 2

www.scholastic.co.uk

Book design by Stephanie Yang

Contents

Bright Burrow
BASIL FOREST
MIRROR LAKE
RADISE BEACH
RADISH HIGH SCHOOL
CUCUMBER ROW
HAY ARENA
CARROT CENTRAL
STRAWBERRY FIELDS

For the Flügels, whose friendship
makes me feel lucky
every day xxx

Not Any Rabbit Hole

This looks like a rabbit hole, right? It's small, round and muddy, with just enough space for a bunny to hop in, burrow around, sleep and eat.

But as you may have noticed, sometimes what seems to be on the outside is very different on the inside. And that's true nowhere more so than here.

For this isn't any rabbit hole. This one holds a special secret. A magical secret.

Inside this rabbit hole is the huge, amazing world of the Lucky Bunnies.

So watch your head, and come on in.

Welcome to the magical land of Bright Burrow...

ONE
At the Tail Salon

It was a sunny Sunday afternoon in Bright Burrow, and Ruby, Sky, Star, Petal and Diamond scampered along the shiny green cobbles of Cucumber Row. The five friends were heading towards their favourite tail salon, Fur Real, where they went every Sunday to have their tails trimmed, brushed and styled.

"Ooh, look!" said Sky, skipping up to a gift shop called Mrs Whiskers's Pawfect Presents. "Bunny balloons!" She pressed her extremely furry head to the window. It was filled with brightly coloured balloons that had been shaped, stretched and tied into floating rabbit figures.

Everyone turned to look at the impressive balloon display, apart from Star who kept striding ahead. "We'll be lucky to get spots at Fur Real if we don't hurry up," she said.

Sky took a last longing look at the balloons, then ran to catch up with her friends.

"I'm sure we can go there later," said Petal when she saw Sky's disappointed face and turned-down whiskers.

They reached the entrance of Fur Real, where glittering disco balls spun across the top of the window. Star pushed open the door, making the bells on it tinkle like a triangle. As she was about to step in, a tiny blur of mint-green fur hurtled past them outside.

"Twinkle?" Ruby called out into the street.

Their friend Twinkle was supposed to meet them earlier that day, but he'd never shown up.

The little mint-green blur skidded to a stop, grinned and did a double backflip over to his friends.

"It's lucky we bumped into you!" said Petal. "Is everything all right?" she asked Twinkle as the friends hopped into Fur Real. The walls were covered in glossy pictures of tails of every size, shape and colour.

"Yes, I'm fine, thanks," Twinkle squeaked. "Furbulous, in fact! Look, that's lucky, too – there are six spare seats for us!"

They took turns dipping their tails in the bathtub full of Bunny Bubbles in the corner of the salon, then jumped up on to the line of toadstool

chairs. Beside each chair stood a smiling salon worker with a comb in one paw and a pair of scissors in the other.

"So where have you been?" asked Ruby as she shook out her wet tail.

"At home, doing a bit of paw-painting," said Twinkle. One of the tail-dressers handed him a Five-Flower Fizz drink, and he took a long, slurping sip through the straw. "I think it might be my very best one yet! Why do you ask?"

"You're late!" said Star, with a twitch of her nose. "We were supposed to meet this morning."

Twinkle flicked his tiny ears up in surprise. "Is it the afternoon already?" he squeaked. "Oh, sorry! I lost track of time. What burrow-tastic adventures did I miss?"

Ruby held up a red paw and counted her four fingers. "So much! We went for brunch at Crocus Café, rode the Clover Train to Paradise Beach, went swimming in Mirror Lake, then had a totally delicious picnic! Diamond even found a magical shell in the sand on Paradise Beach, didn't you, Diamond?"

Diamond leaned over to Twinkle and held out a glowing yellow shell. "It lights up like magic," she said in her shy, quiet voice. "I was so lucky to find it! I'm going to put it on my bedside table at home."

The bunnies often went digging at Paradise Beach, not just because they *loved* to dig, but because sometimes they could find magical surprises hidden in the sand if they searched hard enough.

"What do you call a rabbit who's late?" asked Sky all of a sudden in her chirpy voice.

The friends went quiet while they tried to think of the answer to Sky's joke.

"I've got it!" said Star with a nod. "Paw timing!"

"Nope," said Sky, shaking her fluffy blue head. "Bunny-hind!" Sky thumped her foot as she laughed at her own joke. "Get it? Be-hind... bunny-hind!"

Her friends giggled — everyone except Star. "I think paw timing was better..." Star said. "You know: poor timing?"

"Anyway," Petal said quickly, thinking she'd better change the subject before her friends started arguing. "What is everyone having done

7

today? I've been wondering whether I should get my tail dyed red..."

Twinkle turned to Petal and frowned. "Won't it clash with your pink fur? And your tail is a furbulous colour already, Petal. So pearly-pink! Whereas Star... Star, you could really pull off a red tail. With your yellow body, you'd look like a beautiful bundle of fire!"

"I don't think so!" said Star. "I'm having just a trim and blow-dry, like usual. I want my tail to look perfect for Bounce-a-Lot on Saturday."

Bounce-a-Lot was a festival that took place in Bright Burrow every year, featuring all sorts of bouncing events. Every Lucky Bunny looked forward to it, whether they were chosen as Bouncers to take part in the festival,

or came along to watch the amazing bouncing displays.

"I'd forgotten about Bounce-a-Lot," said Petal, flapping her big ears in excitement. "I don't think I'll be lucky enough to get chosen as a Bouncer, but I don't mind at all. I just love to watch!"

Diamond jumped down from the toadstool chair to check out her tail in the mirror. The tail-dresser had fluffed and combed it into a perfect heart shape.

"That looks absolutely stunning," squeaked Twinkle, putting his paws to his face in admiration. "You're so lucky to have fur like that. I wish mine was thick enough for that style!"

Diamond smiled shyly. "Thanks," she said quietly as she hopped to the door. "See you tomorrow for school?"

"Aren't you coming to Strawberry Fields?" Ruby asked Diamond. "They're showing the film *101 Velveteen Rabbits*. It's supposed to be awesome!" Strawberry Fields was Bright Burrow's theatre and cinema. Next to Paradise Beach, it was one of the friends' favourite places, partly because it served the most delicious strawberry shakes – which refilled like magic whenever a bunny reached the bottom of the cup.

Diamond gave a little shake of her shimmering white head. "No, I can't come tonight. I've got science homework to do. I'll see you in the morning." The bells at the door tinkled as she opened it. She scampered out towards Warren Street, the maze of burrows where all the Lucky Bunnies lived.

"Hey, what do you call a squished strawberry?" chirped Sky. Her eyes twinkled with the thought of her new joke. This time she answered before anyone could guess. "Jam!"

Everyone laughed, the tail-dressers, too.

"That was much better, Sky," said Star. "It was actually quite funny."

"Tell us another one?" Petal asked. She sat forward on her toadstool chair to listen, and her long, drooping ears almost touched the floor.

"Sorry, nope, I can't right now," Sky said. The tail-dresser gave Sky's very furry fur a final brush, and Sky leaped from her chair. She did a dizzying jump and spin in front of the mirror, which undid almost all the tail-dresser's hard work, although Sky didn't seem to notice. "Star has reminded me – I've got to go home and practise my bounce-moves for Bounce-a-Lot," Sky explained. "Mum said she'd buy some hopcorn, too, to help give me extra springing power. Ooh, I can't wait for next Saturday!"

The bells tinkled again as Sky rushed out into Cucumber Row with a hop and a wave.

"Who do you think Mr Nibble will choose to be Bouncers?" said Twinkle as his tail-dresser snipped oh-so-carefully at his tiny little tail. Tomorrow, their teacher at Dandelion School would decide who from their class would be taking part in the Bounce-a-Lot festival.

"Maybe Mr Nibble will choose everyone?" said Petal hopefully. She couldn't bear to see any of her friends disappointed.

"I don't think so!" Star replied. "Only six from each class are chosen. And having everyone wouldn't be fair when *some* bunnies have been preparing for it all year." Star herself was one of those bunnies. She always practised hard, and it paid off – she'd been chosen as a Bouncer every single year so far.

"Life's not always fair," said Ruby with a flick of her curly red whiskers. "It's important to work hard, but sometimes you also need luck!"

TWO
The Oak Class Bouncers

The next morning, Sky woke up extra early with a gigantic smile on her face. She'd dreamed that she'd won the Best Bounce Award at Bounce-a-Lot, after leaping higher than the Weather Rabbit clock tower in Pineapple Square. She jumped out from under her leaf-quilt duvet and ignored the ache in her legs – she'd been practising her bounce-moves until very late last night.

"What would you like for breakfast?" Sky's mum asked. She was in the kitchen, spooning blueberry porridge into six bowls for Sky's younger sisters. They were usually up earlier than Sky, who was the eldest and liked to sleep in, but today she was the first bunny up.

"Ooh, hopcorn, please, Mum!" Sky begged. She did a backflip to the table, knocking a pan off the wall in the process. It clattered on to the floor, and Sky's mum tutted.

"Well, if your sisters weren't awake already, they are now!" Sky's mum said. "And you should really have something more nutritious for breakfast, Sky."

"But, Mum," Sky began, "you know—"

"It's Bounce-a-Lot on Saturday," her mum finished. "Yes, I know. It's all you've been talking about! Just hearing you chatter about all that jumping around has made me feel tired." She poured a bowl of hopcorn for Sky and whispered, "You're lucky your dad's not up yet. Don't tell him I gave this to you!"

Sky winked at her mum and nodded. "Sure thing!" she said. Sky started shovelling the sweet, crunchy hopcorn into her mouth, one

after another. She
liked to see how
many pieces she
could fit in before

she swallowed. Her cheeks grew bigger and bigger as she squeezed more and more of the sweet, crunchy morsels in.

"Guess what – I beat my hopcorn record today," Sky told Diamond on the way to school. They lived in next-door burrows and always skipped to school together. "Twenty-eight pieces!"

Diamond nodded thoughtfully. "Twenty-eight? That's my lucky number. Did you know it's the number of teeth rabbits have?"

"Ooh, really?" said Sky. "I didn't know that. You're so clever, Diamond."

Diamond blushed. "Thanks, Sky. It was actually in our science homework last night."

"Flippety-flop!" Sky put her front paws to her very furry face. "I didn't do the homework!"

"Oh, yes, I'd forgotten you were going to see *101 Velveteen Rabbits*," Diamond said. "Was it good?"

"No idea – I didn't go," said Sky. "I was bouncing all night. Look at my latest move – the lucky high spin!" Sky leaped up so far that

Diamond had to lean backwards to look at her. She spun in the air, a blurry ball of blue fur.

"That was amazing, Sky," Diamond said, clapping her white paws together. "I can't wait to see you perform in Bounce-a-Lot."

They reached the dandelion field that surrounded their school, and ran towards the group of trees in the centre. Each classroom was inside one of the tree trunks, and each class was named after the different trees — Oak Class, Willow Class, Chestnut Class, Pine Class and Maple Class. Sky and Diamond headed for their classroom, in the wide oak tree.

Inside, there were twelve log desks facing their teacher's larger desk and the barkboard behind him. Most of the Oak Class students were sitting at their desks already. Their teacher, Mr Nibble, was almost hidden by the huge lettuce leaf he was busy munching on for his breakfast.

"Knock, knock," chirped Sky as she and Diamond scooted to their desks.

"Who's there?" replied Diamond, Star, Ruby and Petal. Twinkle was missing – he was late, as usual.

Sky grinned. "Lettuce."

"Lettuce who?" Sky's friends asked, playing along with her joke.

"Lettuce in, it's cold outside!" Sky replied, and her friends laughed, even though they'd heard that one before.

"You must have told us that joke a hundred times!" Star complained.

Mr Nibble looked up from his lettuce leaf. The fur on his head folded into a frown. "I see Twinkle's not yet here again, but we should start anyway. Today's an important day." As he took another bite of his breakfast, the tiny form of Twinkle dashed into the classroom.

"Sorry I'm late!" Twinkle squeaked. "Did I miss anything?"

Mr Nibble swallowed his mouthful. "Almost! Now sit down, Twinkle, and please try to be on time. As I was saying, I have an important announcement, which I know you have all been waiting for, so I won't keep you wondering any longer."

Sky nudged Petal at the next-door desk. "Ooh, the Bouncers!" Sky whispered. She sat up as Mr Nibble began reading from a piece of tree bark.

"This year's lucky Oak Class Bouncers for the annual Bounce-a-Lot festival will be ... Star, Toppy, Rainbow, Jewel, Haybury and Twinkle!"

Sky kept waiting and listening. But Mr Nibble had put the piece of bark down. She counted the names on her paws: Star – one, Toppy – two, Rainbow – three, Jewel – four, Haybury – five, Twinkle – six. Sky began to shake. Each class's Bouncer team was always made up of six bunnies. Which meant she hadn't been chosen! Her tummy did a somersault, and she suddenly felt sick from all the hopcorn she'd eaten.

Mr Nibble took another munch of lettuce, then added with his mouth full, "Congratulations, bunnies. You are our Oak Class Bouncers this year! You lucky bunnies will be skipping your lessons this week to practise for Saturday's festival."

Sky was hardly listening. She wasn't a Bouncer! She watched in a daze as Star, Twinkle and the other class Bouncers scampered out of the tree trunk. The rest of the class waved and wished them luck, but Sky couldn't bring herself to move or speak.

Petal reached across and squeezed Sky's paws. "I'm ever so sorry that you weren't chosen," Petal whispered.

"It's OK," Sky managed to reply, but inside she didn't really feel OK. She felt like the unluckiest bunny in Bright Burrow.

That morning's lesson was English, Sky's favourite, but she couldn't concentrate on the spellings Mr Nibble was teaching them. All she could think about was not being in Bounce-a-Lot. What was she going to tell her family? Sky's mum had bought all that extra hopcorn especially for her!

At playtime, Ruby, Petal and Diamond each grabbed a bunch of dandelions from the field and began munching on the yellow flowers, like they did every day at school. But Sky just stood there, looking at the ground.

"Don't forget your dandelion snack," Ruby said. She plucked a pawful of big, yellow dandelions from the ground and held them out to Sky.

Sky smiled at Ruby, took them and nibbled on the petals, but they tasted bitter in her mouth. She let her paw drop to her side.

"Twinkle looked happy to be a Bouncer," said Diamond.

Ruby nodded her glossy red head. "He totally did, didn't he? I think it's his first time!"

Sky twitched her nose and stared at her feet. It would have been her first time, too. She wondered if she'd *ever* be lucky enough to be a Bouncer...

"Sky?" Petal asked politely. "Did you hear what I was saying? Shall we go to Paradise Beach after school?"

"I *so* want to find a glow shell like Diamond's," said Ruby. "Maybe today's my lucky day!"

"Um, OK," said Sky. But she couldn't even get excited about digging in the sand, which she normally loved. She looked up and saw the teams of Bouncers springing around in the far corner of the field. Her heart squeezed as she wished more than anything that she was with them.

THREE
Operation Cheer Up Sky

The next day, Diamond bumped into Petal scampering along Warren Street.

"Where is Sky?" asked Petal, looking around for her fluffy friend. The blue-cobbled road was full of bunnies bounding towards Dandelion School. Petal was so busy searching the masses of bobbing bunny heads for Sky, she didn't see the lamp post right ahead of her. "Ouch!" Petal yelped as she bounced right into it.

"Are you all right?" said Diamond, stopping to help Petal up.

Petal took Diamond's paw and got to her feet. "I'm fine," she said cheerily. "It happens all the time. I'm so unlucky like that!"

Diamond smiled to herself. No one else bumped into lamp posts like Petal did. Diamond thought it was probably because Petal was clumsy, rather

than unlucky. But she didn't say anything, and instead told Petal, "Sky has a toothache."

"A toothache?" Petal repeated. "That's strange. I am positive she said she went to see Dr Molar, the dentist, just last week."

Diamond twitched her white whiskers as she thought. "Sky *has* been eating a lot of hopcorn. Maybe that's given her a bad tooth."

"Maybe," said Petal. "Or perhaps Sky's upset about not being chosen to be a Bouncer."

"But she said she was fine about it yesterday," said Diamond as they walked through the school gates and into the dandelion field.

Petal flicked her long pink ears over her shoulders. "I think she might have been fibbing. Did you notice how she didn't tell one joke yesterday after Mr Nibble announced the team for Bounce-a-Lot? *And* Sky left Paradise

Beach early last night. Perhaps she's upset and she's trying to hide it."

"Oh dear, that's not good!" said Diamond.

"What's not good?" asked Ruby, scampering up behind them in a blur of red.

"Sky," Petal told Ruby. "I think she's miserable that she hasn't been chosen as a Bouncer."

"Really?" Ruby wriggled her curly whiskers, then clapped her paws together. "Then we totally have to work some lucky bunny magic to cheer her up!"

Diamond frowned. If Sky really was so upset about not being in Bounce-a-Lot, how easy would it be to help her get over it?

They reached the school trees and hopped to their desks inside the oak trunk. Today, Mr Nibble was gnawing on a stem of broccoli, and the floor

around him was covered in little specks of green. The classroom wasn't even half full of bunnies, with seven of the desks empty – six places where the chosen Bouncers usually sat, plus Sky's.

The first lesson was food technology, and Mr Nibble put the class into groups to make Berry Bakes. Luckily, Petal was put with Ruby and Diamond – now they could make a plan to cheer up Sky as they worked!

Petal tied back her ears into a bow so they wouldn't droop into the food, and Diamond unhooked three shiny lily-pad aprons from a peg. But Ruby shook her head when Diamond handed one to her. "I don't need an apron!" Ruby told her.

"But Mr Nibble said we had to wear them," Diamond replied quietly.

"That's because he's so messy." Ruby nodded towards their teacher. "He can't even eat broccoli without making a mess. I'll be totally fine." She waved the apron away, and Diamond shrugged and hooked it back up on the tree-trunk wall.

Ruby studied the recipe Mr Nibble had written on the barkboard. "Step one, mash the blackberries." She took a masher from the pot on the cooking bench and began squishing the blackberries in a chestnut bowl. Diamond winced as bright purple blackberry juice squirted all over Ruby's fur, but she didn't seem to notice.

"What's next?" said Petal, squinting. She had the best hearing out of the friends and could

make out the tiniest whisper, but her eyesight wasn't very good and she struggled to see the barkboard.

"We have to add the blueberries," Ruby said, glancing at the recipe again. "Then add torn-up mint leaves and pour the mixture into a baking dish."

While the friends worked, they went back to talking about Sky.

"Can anyone think of some ideas of how we could cheer her up?" Petal asked as she poured the blueberries into the bowl of mashed blackberries.

"There are so many ways!" said Ruby, who liked solving problems. "We should totally write a list!" Ruby also liked lists and had a list for everything, such as her top ten list of favourite foods, her list of every film she'd seen and her list of all the herbs that grew in Basil Forest.

Ruby wiped her paws on the pale red fur of her tummy, spreading blackberry juice everywhere, and took out her exercise barkbook from her desk. "So, what should we try first?"

Diamond pointed at the dish. "Berry Bake is Sky's favourite, right? We could take her this one to try to cheer her up?"

"That's lucky – and an awesome idea!" said Ruby as she scribbled down the first item on the list.

"How about carrots?" suggested Petal. "They're Sky's most favourite vegetable."

"We could take Sky to Carrot Central?" said Diamond. It was a carrot field in Bright Burrow where the vegetables luckily never ever stopped growing, and it was very popular with all the bunnies.

Their Berry Bake was ready to be cooked, so Diamond carried it over carefully to the fireplace in the corner of the classroom. As the tree trunk filled with delicious fruit smells, the three friends focused on writing their list.

By the time the Berry Bakes were ready at the end of the lesson, Ruby had written down four ideas. She closed her barkbook as the school bell rang out, and Petal stuck her paws in her giant ears.

"Sometimes I wish my ears weren't quite so good at hearing," Petal said as the piercing sound made her brain rattle.

"But it's so lucky that you can hear *everything*," said Diamond. "I wish I could. It's much better than having good eyesight." All rabbits could see in the dark, but Diamond's eyes worked even in pitch-black. It sometimes came in handy, but she thought being able to hear even the tiniest whisper would be much better. Then she'd be able to listen to her parents whispering – her birthday was coming up, and she *really* wanted to know what they were getting her.

"So ... who's going to take the Berry Bake to Sky's burrow after school?" asked Ruby.

"I can do it," said Petal as she untied her ears and apron. In fact, she lived the furthest away from Sky, but she knew Ruby had to take her little sister home after school, and Diamond would be rushing back to her burrow to do her homework.

"Thanks, Petal," Diamond said. "I really hope it helps."

Ruby twitched her nose. "Well, we have lots of awesome ideas for Operation Cheer Up Sky. One of them has got to work!"

Petal put her paws to her face. "I hope you're right, Ruby. I can't bear the thought of Sky being sad!"

FOUR
Carrot Central

"Sky!" Sky's dad called gruffly. "Ruby and Petal are here for you."

Sky jolted out of bed. What were her friends doing at her burrow so early? It was a school day, but her parents would have woken her up if she'd slept in.

Sky rubbed the sleep from her fluff-edged eyes

and pulled her yellow Dandelion School tie over her head. She hopped into the kitchen, past the Berry Bake that Petal had brought yesterday. She hadn't felt like eating it, even though it was her favourite. Instead, Sky's sisters had eaten most of it for dessert last night, and by the look of the empty bowl, Dad had had the rest for his breakfast. She began to wonder, *If Dad eats that for breakfast, why can't I have hopcorn?*

She walked past her dad to the hallway, spotting telltale purple berry stains around his mouth. "Hey, Petal. Hey, Ruby. What's going on?" asked Sky. Her two friends were standing at the front door, both hopping from foot to foot.

"It's a surprise," said Ruby.

Sky looked out of the doorway and up at the purple-grey sky. The sun hadn't even risen, although the Luck Rainbow arced across the sky as it always did. Sometimes one of the strips of colour in the rainbow shone more than the others, which meant a certain type of luck was around that day.

Sky yawned. "Do you think the surprise could wait until later? I'm super tired."

"I'm afraid it cannot," said Petal brightly. "But it's a good surprise – you'll see!"

Ruby grabbed Sky's arm with a blackberry-stained paw and pulled her out of the burrow. "Come on – it's awesome. And Diamond is waiting for us!"

"Diamond?" Sky blinked. "Why?"

"Just wait. . ." Ruby kept tugging on Sky's arm until she gave in and started scampering along with them.

They ran down Warren Street's blue cobbles. "Hey, are we going to school?" Sky asked.

"No!" Ruby replied as they reached Sparkle River. Dandelion School was still in the distance.

They hopped across the silver stepping stones that shone in the sparkling water. Often older bunnies swam in Sparkle River, believing it would help keep them young, but it was too early for any bunny to be there yet.

Now they were approaching Bright Burrow's shopping street. "Ooh, Cucumber Row?" Sky guessed again. "But the shops won't be open yet!"

"You're quite right, not Cucumber Row," said Petal. Her giant ears fluttered out behind her as she ran across the green cobbles of the shopping street. She swerved right and two gigantic carrots came into view. These weren't real carrots, but orange-brick towers with green-grass tops on either side of the entrance to Carrot Central.

Sky skidded to a stop. "Carrot Central? But you normally have to line up there all night if you want to get in for the morning. Will we make it before school starts?"

Ruby was standing on tiptoes and squinting at the line. "Awesome . . . there she is!"

Sky followed Ruby's gaze. At first, all she could see was hundreds of bunny ears in all shapes and sizes, but then her eyes fell on two pale pink ears, edged with white fur. Those were Diamond's ears – and luckily it looked as if she was right at the front of the line!

"We wanted to cheer you up," Petal explained. She took Sky's paw and guided her towards Diamond, past the winding line that circled the whole of Carrot Central. The round field was jam-packed with bright orange carrots, and as soon as one was plucked, another would magically spring up in its place. "Diamond's been here since yesterday," Petal continued, "to make

sure you can have as many carrots as you want this morning."

Ruby jumped up and spun on the spot. "And we know how you totally love carrots!"

Sky tried to smile at her friends, even though her stomach felt cold and empty with disappointment. They were being so kind to her, but she just couldn't forget about not being a Bouncer.

As they drew nearer to Diamond, Sky heard her shouting. She frowned – Diamond never raised her voice. She sniffed – what was that funny, eggy smell?

"What do you think you are doing?" Diamond yelled.

They finally reached the front of the queue, and the bunny Diamond was talking to came into view. Except, it wasn't a bunny. . .

It was a ferret! They all recognized Hiss – he was a very annoying ferret who sometimes sneaked into Bright Burrow.

"Hiss, what are you doing here?" Ruby asked. She was pinching her nose, so her voice came out all funny. Like all ferrets, Hiss didn't smell very nice, especially if you had Ruby's super-smelling nose.

Hiss put his little brown paws on his hips and raised himself upwards on his hind legs. Now he towered over the bunnies – even Petal, the tallest of them all. "I am getting some

carrots," Hiss said. "And anyways, what's it to you?"

Diamond looked up at Hiss's angry black-and-white face and backed away. "But . . . but you haven't been queuing all night," she said, then turned to her friends and added, "He just suddenly appeared in front of me."

The bunnies in the queue behind Diamond all nodded and tutted.

"It sounds like you've been up to your tricks again, Hiss," said Ruby, who was still holding her nose with a paw. She looked around at the ground and spotted some fresh earth – as if someone had quickly tried to cover up a hole. "Did you dig a hole to get to the front?"

"Hole?" Hiss stuck his small black nose in the air. "I dunno what you're talking about!"

"What is that then?" asked Petal, flapping an ear at the ground.

"I dunno!" Hiss repeated, not even looking down.

"Yes, you totally do!" said Ruby. "You're a bad liar. Your cheeks have gone red."

Hiss snorted. "They have not!"

"They have too!" Ruby replied. "You just can't see them. You should look in Mirror Lake, then you'll see."

"I will then! I'll show you!" said Hiss, and he lowered his front paws to the ground and darted away past the line of waiting bunnies.

Petal gave Ruby a big smile. "Well done, Ruby. That got rid of him."

Ruby smiled back, making her curly whiskers dance. "Ferrets can be so sneaky," she said, "but they're also not very clever. Luckily he fell for my trick!"

"Thank you, Ruby," said Diamond. "Now Sky can take my place as first in the queue without Hiss bothering her."

Petal pointed ahead. "Look, I think it's about to open!"

The gatekeeper of Carrot Central, a large golden bunny with floppy ears, was hopping through the bright orange field towards them. She unhooked the latch from the carrot-shaped gate and waved Sky in.

But Sky didn't move. She turned to her friends. "Hey, thanks for doing this for me. But the thing is, I really do have a toothache." She put a paw to her jaw where her back tooth throbbed with pain.

Petal was so surprised, her mouth dropped open. "But we thought you were just saying that because you didn't want to come to school after you weren't chosen to be a Bouncer!"

Sky shook her fluffy blue head. "Nope – I went to the dentist again yesterday. Dr Molar said I'd eaten way too much hopcorn."

"Oh, that's unlucky!" Ruby said. "So you're really, totally OK? Even with Star and Twinkle being on the team?"

"Yep," Sky replied. Then a frown appeared on her furry forehead. "You haven't said anything to Star

and Twinkle about this, have you? I don't want to make them feel bad."

"No," said Diamond. "And we won't. We just want you to be happy."

"I am!" Sky insisted, and she tried to ignore the empty feeling in her stomach. The four friends began walking away from Carrot Central. "Hey," Sky said, quickly trying to think of a joke to prove she was OK. "Um . . . what do you get if you cross a carrot with a parrot?"

"What?" Ruby asked.

"Um . . . a carrot-parrot!" said Sky.

Her friends all laughed, but alarm bells were ringing inside Petal's head. That joke was truly awful, which proved only one thing. Sky wasn't really over her disappointment at all.

FIVE
Purple Silkleaf

Later that day at school, Petal scratched a message on a strip of barknote and passed it to Diamond and Ruby. It read:

What shall we do about Sky? I'm worried about her.

"But I thought Sky was OK," Diamond whispered to Petal as they ran outside at playtime. "She told us she was."

Petal flicked a long ear. "Sky says that, but I still think she's fibbing. Her carrot joke this morning didn't make sense at all, and look at how she's staring at the Bouncers practising over there."

Diamond and Ruby turned to look at Sky. She was sitting cross-legged on the grass, her fluffy

head in her paws, her gaze fixed on the Bouncer teams at the other side of the dandelion field.

"I think she just told us she's fine so that we don't worry about her," Petal added.

Ruby thought back to their list. "Then we need to do the next thing on our Operation Cheer Up Sky list," she said. "Number three: Persuade Mr Nibble to let her be a Bouncer after all!"

After school, Sky's dad picked her up to take her to the dentist again, which meant Diamond, Ruby and Petal could work out a plan on their way home.

"We need to speak to Mr Nibble when Sky isn't around," said Diamond as they hopped out of the school gates.

"But how do we do that?" Petal asked. "Sky's always in class with us."

Ruby put a paw to her mouth as she thought through the problem. "I know — we could totally go to his burrow!" she said. "Except ... I don't know where he lives. . ."

"I do!" said Diamond. "I've been there before for some extra maths lessons."

"Extra maths?" said Petal, flapping an ear over her eyes in horror. "Urgh!"

"I like maths," Diamond explained quietly.

Ruby nodded. "Yeah, maths is awesome! Anyway, so luckily Diamond knows where Mr Nibble lives, but how are we going to change his mind about choosing Sky?"

The three friends were silent as they all tried to

think of an idea. In the distance,
the silver Weather Rabbit
in Pineapple Square
suddenly popped out of
his clock tower. "Rain is
coming!" he squealed. "Get
ready for rain!"

The sky had been blue and cloudless, but now rain clouds moved in. The next moment, rain began pattering down on the bunnies. They sped up to a run along Warren Street.

"But we absolutely cannot go home yet," said Petal. She looked up to the grey, rainy sky, with the Luck Rainbow arcing through it. "Oh, it's such bad luck for it to rain, when we have most important Operation Cheer Up Sky work to do!"

"You know the Weather Rabbit," Diamond replied, twitching her pink nose to shake off the raindrops. "He likes to change the weather all of a sudden like that."

As if to prove Diamond's words, the mechanical silver rabbit popped out of the clock tower again. "Sunny, sunny sunshine!" he screeched. "Here comes the sun!"

The rain stopped immediately, and the grey clouds slid away to reveal a bright yellow sunshine in a pale blue sky.

Ruby clasped her red paws together. "So, back to business," she said. "What can we do to persuade Mr Nibble to let Sky be a Bouncer?"

"We could bring Mr Nibble something he likes to eat?" Diamond suggested.

Ruby sniffed. "He likes eating *everything* though!" she said.

"Silkleaf!" Petal shouted. The bunnies nearby turned to look at her, and Petal lowered her voice. "I overheard Mr Nibble talking to Mrs Lop at school about desperately wanting some silkleaf, but he doesn't have any time to go and pick it."

"Then that's totally what we can do!" Ruby did another jump-spin. "We can go and get some right now, and then take it to Mr Nibble before school in the morning."

The three friends hopped off Warren Street, heading for Basil Forest. They crossed the

glossy stepping stones of Sparkle River and then scampered towards Pineapple Square. As they passed the clock tower, Diamond hoped more than anything that they'd be lucky and the Weather Rabbit wouldn't pop out to change the weather to rain again.

They passed the end of Cucumber Row where the street bordered Paradise Beach, and ran across the golden sand alongside Mirror Lake. The turquoise lake water perfectly reflected the giant herbs of Basil Forest, which loomed up ahead of them. It was a beautiful mix of huge plants in every shade of green, orange, pink and purple.

"Right, so the purple silkleaf is over by the mint on the east side of the forest," said Ruby.

Petal raised her little pink eyebrows. "How do you know that?"

"My mum eats heaps of it," Ruby explained. "She says it totally helps stop her fur going grey. She's *always* sending me to get it."

The bunnies started hopping through the forest, heading east. Wonderful herby aromas filled their nostrils as they passed rosemary, coriander, thyme and parsley plants.

"Here we are!" announced Ruby when they reached a large patch of purple. The millions of heart-shaped silkleaves stretched far across the forest floor. They began picking the purple leaves, which were still wet from the rain.

Petal jumped as Diamond squealed and said, "My paws!"

"Whatever is it?" Petal asked, quickly hopping over to her friend. "Did you get stung by something? Does it hurt?"

"No, but I'm going to be in big trouble when my mum sees my fur has gone purple!" Diamond held out her paws. Her beautiful white fur was stained bright purple from the silkleaf.

Petal gasped as she and Ruby looked at their own paws – theirs were just as purple. The patches were worse than Ruby's blackberry stains from making the Berry Bake yesterday!

Ruby shrugged as she plucked another pawful of silkleaf. "Never mind, there's nothing we can do about it now."

"It must have been because the leaves are wet," said Petal. She examined the silkleaf she'd

collected in her paws and tried not to let her ears

dangle in them. "Do you think we have enough?"

Diamond didn't reply. She was still staring at

her purple-splattered white fur.

"I think so," Ruby said. "Let's go home before

it gets dark."

The next morning, Ruby, Petal, and Diamond met before the sun rose. They wanted to visit Mr Nibble without the risk of Sky seeing them.

Ruby lifted their teacher's parsnip-shaped door knocker, and let it clatter against the wooden front door. They waited in the dark and quiet — it seemed no other bunny in Bright Burrow was up yet. After a few moments, Mr Nibble swung open the door. By the light coming from inside his burrow, they could see he was wearing a red stripy nightcap.

Petal heard Ruby giggling. She thought Mr Nibble looked rather silly, too, but she didn't want to get in trouble with their teacher. Especially not today, when they needed his help.

Luckily, Mr Nibble didn't seem to notice Ruby — he was yawning too much for that.

"Is ... ahhhh ... something wrong?" he said sleepily. "Are you ... ahhhh ... in trouble?"

"Oh no," Ruby said quickly. "We just brought you some purple silkleaf!" She held out a moss-weave basket filled with the silkleaves they'd picked. Mr Nibble peered at it with his paws behind his back.

"You could have given this to me at school," Mr Nibble said, still not taking the basket from Ruby.

"Actually, we needed to speak to you outside of school." Petal flapped her huge ears nervously, then added, "Mr Nibble, please will you let Sky join the Bouncers for Bounce-a-Lot?"

Mr Nibble didn't say anything for a moment, but his greying whiskers twitched up and down. Petal hoped that was a good sign.

Finally, their teacher opened his mouth. "I thought you three bunnies were better than that! I will not put Sky in the team just because you brought me silkleaf. You cannot try to bribe me like this!"

Diamond hid behind Petal. She'd never seen their teacher so angry.

"And anyway," Mr Nibble continued, "I like pink silkleaf best, not purple!"

"*Pink* silkleaf? Where does *that* grow?" Petal whispered to Ruby.

Ruby shrugged. It definitely wasn't on her list of herbs that grew in Basil Forest!

At that very moment, the sun rose above the horizon, lighting up Bright Burrow as the new day began. Mr Nibble shrieked and pointed behind them. "What have you done to my garden?"

The friends looked backwards at his neat, green lawn. Except it wasn't so neat and green any more – they'd tracked purple paw prints all over it, and now it looked like a patchwork quilt!

Oh no! thought Diamond. She started rubbing at the grass with her tail, ruining the heart-shape style, but all that did was spread the purple further across the grass. If only she'd kept the dock leaves on her paws that her dad had made her wear last night – he'd taken one look at her when she'd returned from Basil Forest and wouldn't let her enter their burrow without her tying them on!

Now there is no way Mr Nibble will change his mind, thought Ruby. It was such bad luck! "We're so sorry, Mr Nibble," Ruby said.

"But if it rains again, the purple might wash away," Petal suggested, trying to make things better.

Mr Nibble sighed. "Hmm, we'll see! Now leave me to my peace before school starts, and please try to get rid of those fur-stains on your paws between now and then. I don't want my classroom covered in purple prints, too!"

Petal, Ruby and Diamond scampered away carefully, avoiding the lawn, as Mr Nibble ducked back into his burrow, mumbling to himself.

"What are we going to do now?" Petal asked her friends. As she ran, Petal rubbed her front paws together to try to get rid of the stains. "We're back to square one!"

SIX
Dig-a-Lot

"Look at the Luck Rainbow!" said Ruby. She, Diamond and Petal were scampering towards Sparkle River so they could wash themselves, leaving a trail of purple prints on the ground behind them. "The indigo arc on the rainbow is shining so brightly today."

"What does that mean again?" asked Petal. She

could never quite remember which colour meant what.

"Indigo means finding luck – right, Ruby?" asked Diamond as she tipped her white head to the sky.

"It sure does!" said Ruby. She thought back to their Operation Cheer Up Sky list. "Then we

should totally do number four on our list after school: Dig up something magical at Paradise Beach to give to Sky!"

Petal flapped her long pink ears, feeling excited. "Oh yes! We might even find a Wish Star, and then we'll be able to *wish* Sky into being in Bounce-a-Lot."

But the friends had to get through a whole day of school before they could go to Paradise Beach. Mr Nibble was so grumpy he gave them a long and boring history test, while he sat at his desk chewing loudly on celery sticks. Petal could not concentrate with the sound of Mr Nibble's constant munching.

Sky didn't make any jokes all day, and she didn't even notice the faint purple stains that were left on her friends' paws. Even after washing in Sparkle River, Diamond, Petal and Ruby hadn't been able to get rid of the purple completely. But luckily they were no longer leaving paw prints wherever they went.

As Ruby worked on the history test, the memory of Mr Nibble in his red stripy nightcap kept popping into her head, but she tried not to laugh. She didn't want to make him even angrier with her!

After school, Diamond, Ruby and Petal met at Paradise Beach. "Let's start over there," said Ruby, pointing across the golden sand. "It looks as if that spot near the lake hasn't been dug for ages. We totally have a better chance of finding something there."

Petal tied up her ears and began digging right away, kneeling on to the sand and scooping out pawful after pawful. She was faster than Diamond and Ruby, because she had much bigger paws. Soon she'd dug a hole as deep as a tree, and when she peered into it to search for a magical gift, she tipped right in, ears first.

"Oops-a-daisy!" she said from the bottom of the hole, then added, "There's no surprise in here!" Petal clambered out and quickly started a new hole right next to the old one. But she found nothing there either!

Unfortunately, the three friends weren't the only ones at Paradise Beach. It seemed lots of other bunnies had spotted the indigo arc glowing on the Luck Rainbow, and the beach

became crowded with rabbits flinging sand everywhere. Diamond had to keep shutting her eyes to stop grains of sand flying into them, which made digging pretty difficult. It also meant Diamond didn't see Twinkle and Star heading towards them across the beach.

"Hellooooo!" Twinkle called out, and Diamond

opened her eyes at the sound of her friend's high, happy voice. The tiny green shape of Twinkle was hopping towards her, with Star walking much more slowly behind.

"You shouldn't waste your energy jumping around, Twinkle," Star told him. "We've got to save all our bouncing power for Bounce-a-Lot."

Twinkle didn't reply and kept on hopping, skidding to a stop in front of Diamond. "Have you found anything furbulous?"

"How long have you been here for?" Star asked before anyone could reply. She frowned at her sand-covered friends and the gigantic holes they'd made in the beach. "Those holes are enormous!"

"Ages," said Ruby. "Ever since the end of school."

"We've got to find something to cheer up Sky!" said Petal.

Ruby nudged Petal's paw. Petal suddenly remembered that she wasn't meant to say anything to Twinkle and Star about Sky.

"Petal means we were looking for some awesome gifts. For everyone," said Ruby, trying to cover up Petal's mistake. But it was too late. Twinkle was frowning.

"Why does Sky need cheering up?" he asked.

Diamond tried to think of something to say so they wouldn't have to reveal Sky's disappointment. But she didn't want to lie to her friends.

"She's just so very upset about not being a Bouncer!" Petal admitted, and her ears drooped

with the sadness
of it all.

"Oh flippety!"
Twinkle flung
his mint-green paws
into the air. "I've been so busy-busy with
practising I hadn't thought of that! Sky really
wanted to be a Bouncer, didn't she? Poor Sky!"

"We've tried heaps of things to make her feel
better," Ruby explained. "We made a list and
everything! But we haven't been lucky at all."

Star twitched her golden nose. "I can
understand she's disappointed. But I did tell
Sky before that she needed to practise every
day, all-year round, not just a few weeks before
Bounce-a-Lot."

Twinkle glared up at Star. "Not everyone can be like you, Star. I didn't bounce every day, and I was chosen." Twinkle turned to Petal, Diamond and Ruby and squeaked, "Oh, I feel utterly dreadful! I should have been helping you, but all I've been doing is bouncing!"

Petal put a paw around little Twinkle as tears sprung to his eyes. "It's absolutely not your fault," Petal said. "You didn't know."

"But I should have known!" Twinkle sniffed. "Oh, what *are* we going to do?"

"I'm not sure there's much we can do now," said Star gruffly. "Perhaps Sky will be happy enough to watch Bounce-a-Lot. After all, the next best thing to bouncing yourself is to see others doing it."

Twinkle wasn't so sure. He imagined being Sky and how terribly disappointed he'd feel not to be chosen as a Bouncer after wanting to be in the festival so badly. As the friends left the beach to go home for their suppers, Twinkle decided that he had to do *something*. He just had to work out what.

SEVEN
Bounce-a-Lot

It was the day of Bounce-a-Lot. As Diamond, Petal and Ruby hopped towards Hay Arena, Petal could hear the buzz of the crowd even before the stadium came into sight. No one in Bright Burrow ever missed Bounce-a-Lot – if they weren't in it, then they'd be in the crowd watching it instead. But this year there would be one bunny missing. When the bunnies called at Sky's burrow that morning, she had told them her toothache was too bad for her to come. Petal hadn't believed Sky, but she'd insisted she was telling the truth.

The three friends hardly spoke as they hopped along together in the sunshine. Bounce-a-Lot wouldn't be the same without Sky. Sitting in the crowd with her friends, she would talk and joke about what they were watching. Her commentary on the festival events was always so funny, it made Diamond laugh so hard her stomach ached for days afterwards.

The three bunnies passed Carrot Central, which was closed today because of Bounce-a-Lot. Then Hay Arena came into view. The stadium was made of giant haystacks, built up on top of one another, and bunnies could grab pawfuls of the hay to eat while they watched a festival or sports event. Luckily, it meant they never had to get up from their seats for a snack!

Hundreds of bunnies were hopping into the haystack entrance, and chattering loudly about Bounce-a-Lot and what they were looking forward to most.

"I can't wait to see the Team Hop and Skip," Petal heard a little bunny say.

"My favourite is the Super Bounce," his bushy-tailed friend replied. "Last year, a bunny jumped so high, she was just a dot in the sky, remember?"

Ruby, Diamond and Petal scooted through the crowds into Hay Arena, and jumped up the hay

steps inside. There weren't many empty seats
left, but they were lucky enough to find some
towards the top of the stadium, where they had
a great view of the whole arena.

"Look, there's Star," Diamond said, waving a
now-white-again paw at their friend. Star was
warming up on the far side of the grass below

them – doing little star-jumps that made her ears flap up and down like a bird's wings. Star didn't look up, so she didn't see her friends waving at her.

"Is that Twinkle?" asked Ruby, squinting at the centre of the grass field below. All she could see was a tiny ball of mint green darting across it.

"I think so," Diamond replied. "Why's he running so fast? Shouldn't he be saving his energy?"

Petal waved a pink paw. "Oh, you know what Twinkle is like. He cannot sit still for very long at all. And when he's nervous he's much worse."

Ruby nodded her glossy red head to agree with Petal. "He'll be totally fine once it starts. But I so wish he'd look up so we could say hello."

Twinkle kept on scampering around, zooming about faster than the Clover Train. Then he disappeared into the Bouncer Box, a glass-fronted area on one side of the stadium. It was where all the Bouncers sat when they weren't performing.

A marching bunny band strode on to the grass below and began playing the Bounce-a-Lot

theme tune. "Oh, Sky loves this bit," said Petal, missing Sky even more now. "She always sings along!"

The friends bopped their heads to the music, but they weren't as excited as they normally were. They couldn't stop thinking of Sky, sitting in her burrow all alone.

The band marched off the field, and the commentator's deep voice boomed through the speakers. "Welcome, bunnies young and old, to the festival of the year. The one and only hoptastic, fantastic, leaping, jumping Bounce-a-Lot!"

The crowd of bunnies cheered and clapped as the teams ran out on to the grass. The first event was the Team Hop and Skip, where each team took turns performing a dance made up of different bounce-moves. The team from Oak Class did a dance where they all held paws and skipped together in different shapes to spell out the word *LUCK*. They ended in a move where they spun and leaped in a circle at the same time, and Diamond thought they looked just like a hula-hoop spinning in the air.

Next came the Leapfrog, in which each team formed a line, and the bunnies leaped over one another's backs. As soon as the leaper had reached the end of their team's line, they stopped to become a frog, and the bunny at the back of the line began leaping, until everyone in the team had taken a turn. Some of the bunnies did flicks and kicks as they leaped over their

teammates, and Twinkle even somersaulted in the air every time he made a jump.

"Twinkle might be quite small," said Petal, "but he's ever so good at leapfrogging!"

"Next up is the Hoop Bounce!" said the commentator. "Please be patient while we get the hoops set up."

The teams carried out twelve hoops and spread them out around the grass field. Each Bouncer took turns bouncing from hoop to hoop while trying not to land outside them. Star completed her round without making a single mistake.

"That was totally awesome, Star!" called Ruby as the crowd clapped for Star's perfect round.

Bounce-a-Lot continued with the Super Bounce,

where the members of each team stood on one another's shoulders and did one big leap together. It was very tricky – in some of the teams, the Bouncer at the top lost their balance and fell off mid-bounce. In the Oak Class team, Twinkle was at the very top of the Super Bounce, but he managed to hold on as the six Bouncers flew up in the air in one giant jumping tower.

"Excellent work, Oak Class!" shouted Petal as she munched on a pawful of hay.

"Next is the final event," the commentator's voice boomed around the stadium. "This is what you've all been waiting for: the Bright Burrow Bouncy Big Bounce!"

Diamond clapped her paws together. "This is my favourite!" She felt a jolt of sadness when

she remembered it was the one Sky liked the
most, too.

Twinkle suddenly appeared on the hay step in
front of them.

"What are you doing here?" Ruby asked him.

"Is everything quite all right?" said Petal.

Twinkle was looking around at the steps, as if he'd lost something. "Where's Sky?" he squeaked.

Diamond gave a sigh. "She wouldn't come," Diamond told Twinkle sadly. "She said she still has a toothache."

"What? No-no-no! I need her!" said Twinkle in an even squeakier voice.

"Why?" asked Ruby, twiddling a curly whisker. "Is something wrong? Is everyone on the team OK?"

Twinkle wrung his paws together. "Yes, we're fine. But I'd organized something furbulously special for Sky so that she could be a part of Bounce-a-Lot after all – and now she's not here!"

EIGHT
The Surprise

"Oh dear!" said Petal, flapping her ears furiously.
"We could run back to Warren Street to get her,"
she suggested, but Twinkle was shaking his tiny
head.

"There's simply no time for that," he
squeaked. "The Bright Burrow Bouncy Big
Bounce is about to begin... Oh, and it was

such a fantabulous surprise, too, even if I do say so myself!"

"That's such bad luck," said Ruby. "What was it?"

But Twinkle didn't reply. He was staring at something at the back of the haystacks.

The bunnies turned to look. Diamond could see something fuzzy and blue in the shadows.

"Sky?" Twinkle said. "Is that you?"

The fuzzy blue thing hopped forward slowly.

It *was* Sky! She smiled in a sheepish way and said, "Hey. I'm sorry. I didn't think I wanted to come. But then

I realized that there was no way I could miss Bounce-a-Lot, even if I'm not in it."

"Have you been watching all this time?" asked Petal. "Why didn't you come and sit with us?"

Sky shrugged. "I guess I was embarrassed," she said. "As soon as you left my burrow earlier, I knew I was being silly. I followed you here and found a spot at the back where you wouldn't see me."

The commentator started speaking again before anyone could reply. "Take your places, Bouncers, for the final event: the Bright Burrow Bouncy Big Bounce!" Excited murmurs buzzed all around Hay Arena.

"Oh flippety-flop!" squealed Twinkle. "I've got to go. Sky, you have to come with me!"

Twinkle grabbed Sky's paw and began leaping down the haystack steps, dragging Sky behind him. "What's going on?" Sky asked, feeling very confused as Twinkle pulled her along. There was no way she'd be able to join in Bounce-a-Lot as a Bouncer now. It was far too late.

They reached the field where a large, round trampoline had been placed in the centre. But Twinkle didn't stop – he kept on running, tugging Sky behind him, all the way across the grass and up the steps on the other side of the stadium.

"Hey, Twinkle, where are we going?" panted Sky, feeling very hot under her thick blue fur. For a tiny bunny, Twinkle could run *very* fast.

Finally, Twinkle stopped on a haystack step, and beckoned Sky into an area next to the Bouncer Box. Inside, a huge grey bunny – even bigger than Petal – stood in front of a microphone. "That's lucky, Twinkle, you're just in time," the bunny said in a deep, booming voice. "Is this your friend?"

Twinkle nodded and squeaked, "Yes! This is Sky. Sky, this is Chatsworth, the commentator."

Chatsworth grinned, making his long grey whiskers stretch out wide. "And now, Sky, it's over to you!" He hopped aside.

"What do you mean?" Sky chirped.

Twinkle was bouncing from foot to foot and beaming so hard his smile reached his ears. "Sky,

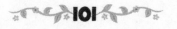

you're going to do the commentary on the last event!" Twinkle explained. "How furbulous is that?"

Sky stared at Twinkle, then at the microphone, then at Chatsworth, then back to Twinkle again. "No way! Really? You don't mind, Chatsworth?"

Chatsworth shook his head. "I've spoken so much today that I've almost lost my voice. I'm very happy for you to do it!"

"And this way you can still be in Bounce-a-Lot, even if you're not bouncing!" Twinkle said, then he paused and put a paw on Sky's arm. "I mean, if you want to," he added.

Sky stared at the microphone some more. "I'd LOVE to!" she yelled.

Twinkle did a jump and spin of happiness.

Chatsworth clapped his large paws together. "You'd better get started. The teams are waiting!" He showed Sky where to stand and how to speak into the microphone. "Just press this button when you're ready," he said.

Sky took the deepest of breaths and tried not to think too much about the hundreds of bunnies in the crowd. Instead, she imagined she was talking about the events to her friends, just like normal.

"Bunnies young and old," Sky began, remembering how the commentator always started. "Are you READY? Are you STEADY? It's time for the final event – the Bright Burrow Bouncy Big Bounce!"

Everyone in the stadium squeaked and clapped
and cheered as the teams lined up behind the
huge trampoline. Chatsworth held up a piece of
barknote for Sky to read.

"The first Bouncer to try her luck on the
trampoline is Star," Sky announced as she read
the first name on the list. "Will Star reach for

the stars, bunnies?" The crowd laughed at Sky's joke as they looked down at the golden figure of Star hopping on to the trampoline. Star strode to the middle, crouched down carefully, and then sprung . . . up, up, up, she went – even higher than the walls of Hay Arena.

"Ooh, what a *start!*" said Sky into the microphone. "Get it: Star-t?" Some of the crowd laughed, and some of the crowd groaned, but everyone was smiling. Sky's fluffy fur prickled with excitement. This was the best surprise ever, and actually *more* fun than being a Bouncer, because she loved talking and telling jokes even more than she loved jumping. She felt like the luckiest bunny in Bright Burrow. Sky continued with her commentary, including as many jokes as she possibly could. When a white bunny with a red tail did his bounce, Sky made a joke about him looking just like a rocket with his tail as the flames. And when it was Twinkle's turn, Sky compared him to a fluffy green firework, which made Twinkle laugh while he was still mid-bounce!

After the last Bouncer had bounced, and the crowd had stood up and cheered all the fantastic teams, Chatsworth showed Sky another barknote. "It's time for the Best Bouncer Team award," he explained in his deep voice.

Sky looked at the note and nearly squealed. She leaned forward into the microphone again and said, "Bunnies young and old, the Best Bouncer Team award this year goes to..." Sky paused, and every single bunny in the stadium waited in silence until she continued, "The Oak Class team!"

Hay Arena erupted into cheers. On the field below, Twinkle, Star and the other Bouncers from their class high-pawed one another. It was an extra-special moment, because their class had never won the award before.

"It means your whole class gets to go to the Bounce-a-Lot after-party at Carrot Central," Chatsworth said. "But before you go, I wanted to say very well done. You did an excellent job on the commentary. If you're not a Bouncer next year, how about we do it together?"

Sky hopped with happiness. "Ooh, I'd love to!" she said, and threw her fluffy blue arms around Chatsworth's legs. "Thank you for letting me join in today."

Sky waved goodbye to Chatsworth and then scampered down from the commentary box to find her friends. Diamond, Ruby and Petal were waiting for Sky at the entrance of Hay Arena.

"You were exceptional!" said Petal. She gave Sky such a strong hug that Sky could hardly breathe, pressed up to Petal's tummy fur.

When Petal finally let go, Ruby and Diamond lifted their paws and Sky high-pawed them both at the same time.

"Are you sure I was really OK?"

asked Sky, twitching her nose. "I mean, I had the best time, but what about everyone in the crowd? It wasn't boring, was it?"

"Boring?" said Diamond. "No! You made it even more fun than normal."

Ruby put her mouth to Sky's ear and whispered, "You were way better than the usual commentator. He totally gets bunnies' names wrong, but you didn't make any mistakes!"

They reached the giant carrot towers of Carrot Central. For once, there was no queue around the circular field, and the bunnies were let straight in at the gate when they said they were in Oak Class. "Ooh, bunny balloons!" Sky chirruped as she spotted multicoloured balloon rabbits tied up all around the field.

"Maybe we'll be lucky enough to each take one home!"

As soon as they were inside, they crouched down and pulled up a carrot in each paw. By the time the friends started munching on the sweet, crunchy carrots, new ones were already growing in their places.

"Hey, this is amazing," Sky declared as a bunny waiter offered her a piece of carrot crunch cake.

She thanked him, took the cake in one paw, and pulled up another carrot from the ground with the other. Another one popped up in the same place immediately.

"Look, there's Star and Twinkle." Diamond pointed across the field with one of her carrots. Their two friends were skipping towards them.

They congratulated Twinkle and Star on a fantastic Bounce-a-Lot. "You were wonderful!" Sky said to them both.

"You were an excellent commentator!" Star told Sky.

"Did you enjoy it, Sky?" Twinkle squeaked.

"I loved it!" Sky said, through a mouthful of carrot. "Thank you!"

"Wait a minute," said Ruby, her brown eyes peering at Sky strangely. "What about your toothache?"

Sky looked down at the carrot in one paw and the cake in the other. "Ooh, it's disappeared," she said. "That's lucky!"

You're in luck!

Read on for a sneak peek
at what the hoppiest, floppiest,
pluckiest, luckiest bunnies around
are getting up to next!

ONE
Invitations

Petal couldn't stay still as she sat behind her log desk at school on Monday morning. Her fluffy pink tail twitched and her long, floppy ears flicked from side to side.

"Petal, do you need the bathroom?" Mr Nibble asked from his desk at the front of the classroom. As usual, the teacher was eating

something. Today, it was a parsnip almost the size of him.

"No, no!" Petal squeaked. "Not at all. I am absolutely fine!"

From her desk next to Petal, Diamond frowned. Petal didn't look fine. It wasn't that she looked unhappy. In fact, she was smiling. She just looked as if she was bursting to do something! Diamond wondered what it might be.

She didn't have to wait long to find out. When the bell rang for playtime, Petal hopped from her desk as if there were a firework under her tail. She called to her friends to follow her out from their classroom, which was inside a large oak tree trunk.

"Diamond, Ruby, Star, Twinkle and Sky, come on!" Petal pulled on her friends' paws to drag them outside. The six bunnies scampered out into the dandelion field that surrounded Dandelion School. The school was made up of five classes – with each classroom inside the trunk of a different tree.

"Ta-da!" Petal said, and she held up five things

high above her pink head. As Petal was the tallest of the friends, the others couldn't quite see what they were.

"Ooh, is it a magic trick?" Sky asked. She flipped into the air to get a better look and saw there were five dock-leaf envelopes in Petal's paws.

Petal shook her head, making her gigantic floppy ears flap around her. "No, it's not a magic trick – they're invitations!"

Twinkle clapped his tiny mint-green paws together. "Invitations?" he squealed. "How furbulous! What are they for?"

Petal brought down her paws and passed the envelopes out to her friends. "You'll have to open them to find out!" she said.